When I Love You
at Christmas

For Kate-DB
For Nigel, with love-TA

NOV   2013

First American Edition 2011
Kane Miller, A Division of EDC Publishing

Text copyright © 2010 David Bedford
Illustrations copyright © 2010 Tamsin Ainslie
First published in Australia by Little Hare Books
First published in the United States of America by Kane Miller in 2011
by arrangement with Australian Licensing Corporation

$9.99

Library of Congress Control Number: 2010941087

Printed through Phoenix Offset
Printed in Shen Zhen, Guangdong Province, China, April 2011
1 2 3 4 5 6 7 8 9 10
ISBN: 978-1-61067-039-5

When I Love You at Christmas

By David Bedford

Illustrated by Tamsin Ainslie

Kane Miller
A DIVISION OF EDC PUBLISHING

When you wrap your gifts
When you tie the bows
That's when I love you

When you mix the bowl
When you smudge your nose
That's when I love you

When you twist the strings
When you hang the star
That's when I love you

When you sing your songs
When you dance and bow
That's when I love you

When you make your cards
When you spell your words
That's when I love you

When you try to sleep
When you toss and turn
That's when I love you

When you wake so fast
When you run and shout
That's when I love you

When you shake and guess
When you whoop and jump
That's when I love you

When you give your gift
When you say "for you"
That's when I love you

When you hold me tight
When you lift me high ...

That's when I love you at Christmas